Dan Daley
P9-EKR-389

THE LAST MINUTE MIRACLE

BERNARD PALMER

Tyndale House
Publishers, Inc.
Wheaton, Illinois

Bernard Palmer is also the well-known author of the Breck Western Series and My Son, My Son. *He lives with his wife, Marjorie, in Holdrege, Nebraska.*

The Danny Orlis Adventure Series

The Final Touchdown
The Last Minute Miracle
The Race Against Time
The Showdown
The Case of the Talking Rocks
The Sacred Ruins

Previously published by Moody Press under the title *Danny Orlis Changes Schools.*

First Tyndale House printing, February 1989
Library of Congress Catalog Card Number 88-51652
ISBN 0-8423-0558-0

Printed in the United States of America

Contents

ONE
Bad news

Danny Orlis picked up his outboard motor and started down the long, narrow dock to the place where his boat was tied. The first faint wisps of dawn were stealing through the trees, and the lake lay like a soft gray mirror before him. He stopped for an instant and took a deep, lingering breath.

Ronald, one of the twins his folks had adopted back in Iron Mountain, Colorado, the spring before, moved up beside him and took hold of his free hand.

"Boy, it's good to have you back, Danny!" Ron said. "Roxie and I got so lonesome for you!"

"Maybe you think I haven't been lonesome for you and the folks and the lake, too," Danny answered. "That trip to Mexico with Aunt Mabel took just about all summer."

"And it won't be very long until you'll have to go away again," Ron said, his voice tinged with disappointment. "We're sure going to miss you."

"I wish I didn't have to go," Danny said. "I'd like to stay here all the time."

He fastened the outboard motor to the back of one of the fishing boats and took the tackle that Ron handed to him.

"Do you suppose Roxie would like to go along?" he asked.

"She said last night she would," Ron replied, "but you know how girls are."

"Go and scratch on her screen," Danny said. "If she wants to go with us, she'll have to get around."

"OK," Ron replied, jumping lightly out of the boat and racing up the path.

"Be quiet about it," Danny warned.

But Ron didn't hear him. "Roxie!" the twin called. "Get up if you want to go fishing with Danny and me!"

"Say, young man!" Mr. Orlis called from the upstairs bedroom. "Be a little quieter. Do you know what time it is?"

"I'm sorry, Dad."

"Put a muffler on that foghorn of yours the next time you let go with it at 4:30 in the morning."

By this time Roxie was up and dressed and halfway out to the boat.

Danny started the motor and headed toward Little McCoy Island out in the center of Angle Bay.

They had reached the place where they were going to fish. Danny cut the motor to trolling speed and helped Roxie get her line into the water. They caught five or six fat walleyes in the next hour, and then Danny headed over to the Ontario mainland to fish for northerns, or jack fish as the people on the Angle called them.

"Why don't we go down to the schoolhouse, Danny?" Ron asked. "I haven't been there for a long time."

"You haven't?" he echoed. "Where have they been holding Sunday school and church?"

"We haven't been having any," Roxie put in.

"How come?" Danny cut the motor so he wouldn't have to shout above its roar. "We used to have some great times in Sunday school and church over there."

"There wasn't much of anybody coming excepting us," Ron explained. "Mr. and Mrs. Jenkins went down to the city to stay with the Jones family, and the Watkins sold out and moved away. Nobody else came regularly at all."

"That's too bad," Danny said.

"Of course, we have our Bible reading and devotions every day," Roxie added.

"I know," Danny told her. "But it doesn't seem right somehow not to have church on Sunday."

"Daddy and Mother tried awfully hard," she went on. "They made all sorts of calls to try to get people interested. We even went over to the schoolhouse five or six Sundays in a row, but no one else showed up."

"Dad said that some of the others might come along once in a while if we had a little group that was meeting regularly," Ron said. "But they won't come now, because they figure that no one else will be there."

"He's still working on it though," Roxie assured him. "And so is Mother."

Danny knew his folks well enough to know that was true. He knew, too, that his dad would have kept the Sunday meetings going if there had been any possible way of doing it.

He looked at Ron and Roxie. They needed the Sunday school, and they needed to hear messages explaining and teaching from the Word of God in addition to family devotions. That was something he would have to be thinking and praying about.

The northerns were not hitting too well, and they had only hooked two or three by the time the boat came in with the mail, and none of them were large enough to keep.

"What say we go in?" Danny suggested. "I might have a letter from Larry telling about our football team. Some of the guys were going to get together and start practice early."

"Suits me," Ron answered, reeling in his line.

There was a letter from Iron Mountain, all right, but it wasn't from Larry. It was from Larry's mother.

"Did you know that Aunt Lydia had a very serious operation two or three weeks ago, Danny?" Mrs. Orlis asked, looking up from reading the letter. "She'll be in the hospital for at least two more weeks, and she won't be able to do her own housework for five or six months."

"Say," Danny answered, "that's tough."

She turned back to the letter and read aloud, "Bob will be away at college, so I won't have to worry about him, but there will be Danny and Larry and Claude to cook and wash and clean for. We haven't decided yet just what to do. . . ."

Mrs. Orlis stopped reading.

"Danny," she said, "you won't be able to go back to Iron Mountain to school. Aunt Lydia won't be able to take care of Larry and Claude without hiring help. We just can't burden her with someone else."

"That's right." Danny could feel the color draining from his cheeks. "What are we going to do?"

"I just don't know," she answered woodenly.

"Maybe I could go down to Warroad or Baudette to school," he suggested. "I'd like that anyway. I could be close to home that way."

By this time his father had come over and joined them.

"I don't know whom you could stay with in either town," Mr. Orlis said. "The Martins couldn't possibly make room for you, and there isn't anyone else we know whom we would feel as though we could impose upon."

"There's Thief River Falls," Danny said. "Some of the guys from here go to school down there."

Mr. Orlis took his watch from his pocket absent-mindedly and held it in his hand.

"There are a lot of good places that you could go, Danny," he said, "but frankly, we've been to quite a lot of expense in getting the twins, and the tourist season wasn't too good. This matter of money for any school is going to be hard."

Danny Orlis nodded solemnly. They had always had everything they really needed up at Angle Inlet, but money wasn't always plentiful. And now there were two more to feed and care for. It was going to be a problem.

"Maybe I could stay out of school and work a year, Dad," he said reluctantly.

"I'd hate to have you do that," his dad replied. "We'll see how things work out."

"It's something that we're going to have to do a good deal of praying about," his mother said.

Jim was ready to go over to Bear River with the mail boat to deliver a load of lumber, and he asked Danny to go along.

"Sure thing," Danny said, trying to put away the ache that was growing in his heart.

"Maybe Ron and Roxie would like to ride with us," Jim said.

"Just a minute and I'll get them."

The twins had been standing on the dock with everybody else a minute or two before.

"Ron!" he called. "Roxie!"

"I haven't seen them in the last few minutes, Danny," his dad answered.

"I'll go down to the cabins," Danny said to Jim. "It will only take a minute."

He ran down to the tourist cabins along the creek, but there was no sign of the twins. The boat was still tied to the dock. They hadn't taken that. And Laddie was lying in the shade of the towering pine tree by the front porch. Usually he went with them wherever they went.

Danny went back to the little log barn where he kept his rabbits, and into the store and post office beside it, but they weren't there.

"Where do you suppose they could be, Mother?" he asked, stopping at the kitchen door.

"I don't know."

Concern was quick in her face. The forests and muskeg stretched for miles in every direction around their house and buildings, and the twins weren't yet accustomed to the dangers of the Angle country.

"Do you suppose we ought to go and look for them?" she asked.

"Jim and I'll go, Mother," Danny told her. "We'll take Laddie."

He called to the big dog and Jim.

"Where do you suppose they'd be apt to go?" his friend asked as they stood together on the edge of the clearing.

"Say," Danny exclaimed, "I just remembered that Ron and Roxie asked me to take them over to the schoolhouse. You don't suppose that's where they started, do you?"

"It could be," Jim answered. "Ron wanted me to go over there with them on our last trip."

Danny and Jim and Laddie started up the narrow, twisting trail toward the schoolhouse.

"They've been along here, all right," said Danny. "There are broken twigs on the ground, and over here is the wrapper off a stick of gum."

"They don't have too much of a head start on us," Jim said. "We ought to catch up with them before long."

They walked for fifteen or twenty minutes along the trail when Danny Orlis stopped suddenly.

"Did you hear that?"

"Hear what?"

"It—it sounded like a scream for help!"

TWO
A cry for help

Danny stood there for a moment or two, scarcely daring to breathe. A shiver of fear ran up his spine. "Did—did you hear that, Jim?" he managed again. "Did you hear someone scream?"

"I think so," his companion answered uncertainly. They listened again. "But I don't know where it came from."

And then it came again: a soft, plaintive wail of terror from out in the muskeg to the left of the trail.

"There!" Danny exclaimed. "Did you hear it that time?"

"It sounded like Roxie!"

They heard it again. "Help! Help!"

"It's Roxie, all right," Danny said. His heart was pounding in his throat, and the palms of his hands were moist with perspiration. For a split instant he could not move.

She screamed again. The hair raised on the back of Laddie's neck, and a low, ominous growl escaped his throat. The big dog turned, took two or three steps off the trail, then stopped and sniffed the air.

"It's the twins!" Jim cried. "They must be in trouble!"

With that, Laddie and the two boys went plunging into the muskeg in the direction of the screams!

"We're coming!" Danny Orlis shouted as loudly as he could. "We're coming!"

It was hard going in the thick tangle of brush and swamp grass and water. Two or three times Danny caught his foot on a dead-fall and went sprawling into the brush and muck. His arms and face were scratched and bleeding, and he had a long gash on his leg where a sharp, broken branch raked him as he fell. But he did not stop. He dared not. Jim was right beside him.

"Help!" Roxie cried again.

They were closer this time, close enough to hear the full terror of her voice.

"We're coming, Roxie!" Danny shouted to her.

Something must have lured the kids off the path and out into the muskeg, something that had turned on them. And then Danny heard it: the low, rumbling snort of an angered cow moose.

He knew in an instant what had happened. The kids had seen her calf and had tried to get close to it. Finally they had managed to get between her and the little one. And she had charged, or was about to.

"Hurry!" Roxie sobbed. "Hurry, Danny! Hurry!"

At that instant he caught a glimpse of the big, ugly animal through the trees. She was standing at the base of a huge oak, snorting and pawing her anger. And perched precariously among the branches, just beyond the reach of her massive head, clung Roxie. Ron was a little higher in the same tree. The moose butted the tree savagely with her head, and Roxie screamed again.

"Sic 'em, Laddie!" cried Danny. "Sic 'em!"

The big dog had seen what was happening and had already bounded through the brush toward the bad-tempered moose. With a wild exultant cry of battle that caused the moose to whirl quickly to face him, Laddie leaped for her tender nose. She shook him off with a scream of pain. But he scrambled nimbly to his feet and leaped at her again, half rolling in the air to avoid her slashing hoofs.

"Sic 'em, Laddie! Sic 'em!" Danny ordered.

By this time the cow moose had forgotten Ron and Roxie in the tree, had forgotten everything except the brown bundle of fury that had attacked her so suddenly.

"Sic 'em, Laddie! Take her away!" Danny ordered, motioning with his arm.

The dog dropped back instantly at the command and, snarling and yipping, nipped at her heels. With a wild bellow to her calf the cow lumbered off through the woods. The clumsy calf staggered along behind.

"Oh, I'm so glad you came!" Roxie said over and over again as Danny and Jim helped her and Ron out of the tree. "I'm so glad you came."

"That old moose almost got us," Ron gasped. Fright was still evident in his voice. "If we hadn't climbed that tree when we did, she would have. And all we did was to try to pet her baby calf."

"That's just about the worst thing you can try to do," Danny told him, "to get a cow moose, or any other kind of mother animal riled up. Start fiddling with their babies and you're in trouble."

"Believe me, I'll never do that again!" Ron vowed fervently.

"You'd better not go off into the woods alone again either," Danny said, "until you're old enough and know your way around so that you can take care of yourselves."

"Don't worry," Roxie answered, "we won't. We prayed and prayed, but we—we got to wondering whether God heard our prayers when no one came."

"God always hears our prayers," Danny said to her. "The only thing is that he doesn't always answer them exactly the way we expect, or maybe want him to."

"I know that," she said quickly. "I—"

"Say," Jim cut in, "I hear that calf stumbling around out there in the brush. We'd better be getting on our way. That old mama moose might be coming back here any time."

"That's right," Danny replied.

"But what about Laddie?" Ron asked.

"Don't you worry about him," Danny laughed. "He'll chase that moose until he knows we've had time to get out of here. Then he'll leave her and come home. He'll probably be lying on the back steps waiting for us when we get there."

That night Danny prayed for a long while about getting to high school the following month. The tuition would be paid by the school district, and there was a small allowance for having to stay away from home. But it wasn't nearly enough to take care of all the expenses. It was no wonder that his dad was concerned about it.

"Dear Lord Jesus," he prayed. "You know all the problems that are troubling us. You know about this matter of getting to school, and how badly I want to go this year. Help us to work it out, if it is your will. But if it is your will that I stay home this year, help me to do it without complaining. Amen."

The following morning was Sunday, and Danny slept a little longer than usual. Ron and Roxie were already up and dressed when he came downstairs with his shoes in his hand.

"We thought that you must be going to sleep all morning," Roxie said with a smile, coming over and sitting close beside him.

"Not me," Danny said good-naturedly, "you were just lucky to beat me out of bed this morning."

"Boy," Ron put in after a moment or two, "I sure wish we were going to get to go to Sunday school today! That's the one thing I miss about Iron Mountain the most."

"We're going to try our best to get our Sunday school and church going again," Mr. Orlis said. "I miss it, too."

"So do I," Danny's mother added.

"I've been thinking a lot about that," Danny said. "It would be a lot better to go to a regular Sunday school, I know. But as long as we can't, why don't we have Sunday school ourselves?"

"What do you mean, Danny?"

"We could have our own," he repeated. "One of us could lead us in singing some choruses and hymns we all know, and someone else could read Scripture and lead in prayer. Then you could teach us a lesson out of the Bible, Dad."

"That sounds like fun," Roxie declared excitedly. "I'd like to lead the singing."

Mr. Orlis sat there a moment or two, tugging at his ear. "I think you've got something there, Danny," he said. "I don't know why we didn't think of that before."

Mrs. Orlis had come into the room by this time. "I think I've got a few of the songbooks we used to use over at the schoolhouse," she said, starting toward the downstairs bedroom. "And there may be an old quarterly or two."

They sang half a dozen choruses and old familiar hymns with Roxie keeping time to the music with her dainty little hands. Then Danny read Scripture, and Ron led in prayer. Mr. Orlis chose the story of Nicodemus in the third chapter of John and taught it, stopping every now and then to ask questions.

When they finally finished, Roxie, who was curled quietly on Mrs. Orlis' lap said, "You know, that was just about the nicest Sunday school I've ever been to."

"It was nice, wasn't it?"

"I was just thinking," Ron put in. "There are lots of special things we could do. We could have a time for learning memory verses and just regular Scripture, and maybe we could have a quiz on the last week's lesson."

"And we could take turns praying," Danny said, "so we can all learn to pray in public."

"This is going to be lots of fun."

"There's just one thing wrong," Mrs. Orlis said, looking up at the clock. "We ought to have church, too. The Sunday school is fine, but Sunday isn't really Sunday without a church service."

"Now listen, Mother," Danny's dad protested, "I agree with you on that, but don't look at me. I can't preach a sermon."

"I don't expect you to," she laughed. "But we can all sit quietly and listen to a radio pastor. There's an awfully good one who comes on in a few minutes over the Winnipeg station."

Mr. Orlis turned on the radio, and they all sat quietly as the radio pastor came on.

The next day was Monday, and Tex Williams flew out with the mail and supplies. When he went back to Baudette, Mr. Orlis rode along.

"I want to find out what I can about a school for you, Danny," he said. "If I can't get any satisfaction at Warroad or Baudette, I'll have Tex fly me down to Black Duck or Bemidji."

Carl Orlis came back on the boat the next afternoon. Danny could see by the somber look on his face that he didn't have good news.

"It's not very hopeful, Danny," Mr. Orlis said. "There are good schools in Baudette and Warroad, of course, but I couldn't find anyone in either town who could take you that I'd want you to stay with."

"What are we going to do, Dad?" Danny asked softly.

"I don't know," Mr. Orlis replied. "I don't know."

Danny looked over at the twins. And for the first time a bit of jealousy crept into his heart. If it weren't for them, he wouldn't have any problem about going to school. There would be plenty of money for his board and room.

THREE
Answered prayer

Danny Orlis didn't sleep very well that night. Every time he closed his eyes, he could see the school at Iron Mountain and the kids that he had been in class with. Larry and the gang would be registering in the morning. Then the football team would report down at the gym for their uniforms and equipment and would go charging out onto the field for their first practice session.

Danny swung his legs over the side of the bed and sat up. It was going to be tough staying at home for the winter when he wanted to go to school so badly. Strange how often he thought that he hated school, and had looked forward to the day when he wouldn't have to go anymore! Now that he was faced with the prospect of staying at home, there was a big empty void in his heart.

It was not that he blamed his folks for it, or the twins either, for that matter. He was glad that Ron and Roxie were in the family now. It was good having a brother and sister.

But, how he wanted to go on to school! And going away from home was so terribly expensive. He sighed deeply.

The following morning at the breakfast table the whole family prayed about it. Roxie came over after they had finished and put her arm about his shoulder tenderly.

"I sure hope you get to go on to school, Danny," she said, her eyes big and glistening with tears. "I've been praying for you all the time. I just know that God is going to work it out somehow."

A sharp pain drove into his heart. To think that he had even been a little jealous of her and Ron—that the day before he had been angry because his folks had to spend money feeding and clothing the twins that could be used to help him get to go on to high school! He put his arm about Roxie and squeezed her hard.

"Thanks a lot, honey," he smiled. "Everything will work out exactly the way God wants it to. You don't need to worry about that."

But even though he knew what he said was true, that deep throbbing ache was still in his heart.

After breakfast he and Ron went out and started to straighten his traps and get them ready for the trapping season that was just ahead. They didn't even hear the mail boat come into the creek until Cap blew the whistle as he edged the little boat up to the dock.

"Come on, Danny," Ron said, jumping to his feet, "let's go and see Jim."

Danny got up slowly.

"Jim won't be along," he said, more to himself than to Ron. "He started school today."

"And Roxie and I start in the morning," Ron said, his voice rising. "Cap was supposed to bring us our school supplies on this trip. I sure hope he did."

"If Cap promised to do it, he's got them," Danny called after his young brother.

Ron had already run out onto the dock and jumped nimbly into the boat. When Danny got there, Ron had already ripped the paper off the package that Cap had brought for him.

Danny picked up the mail sack and carried it back to the post office, and his dad began to sort it.

"Another one of those pink envelopes from Mexico," Mr. Orlis grinned, handing it across the counter to Danny. "You must have done all right on that trip down there this summer from the way the mail's been coming in."

Danny felt the color come up into his cheeks as he took the letter and opened it. It was from Kay all right. He could tell by the handwriting.

"Hey, Roxie," Ron called. "Danny got a letter from his girl."

"Take it easy, fella," he grinned, "or I'll dump you in the lake by your heels."

"Can I read it, Danny?" Ron persisted. "Can I?"

"Get along with you," Danny told him. "I haven't even read it myself."

"You always let us read your other letters—the ones you get from Larry and the guys back in Iron Mountain," his adopted brother went on.

"But this is different," Danny answered.

Kay was just a good friend he had met in Mexico that summer, the daughter of a missionary who served with his Aunt Mabel. But he didn't want the

kids, or anyone else reading what she had written.
He went out of the post office and around the corner where he opened the letter.

By the time you get this, I'll be in Minnesota going to school. Your Aunt Mabel wrote up to Cedarton, Minnesota, for me. That's where the church is that gives most of her support. She wrote to the pastor and asked if there was a family in the congregation who would let me board and room with them while I went to high school. You should have seen the letters that we got. I don't know just yet which place I'll stay. There were so many. . . . Of course, I'm going to have to work for my room and board, but I don't mind that. The important thing is to be able to go to school.

Danny read the letter through again slowly. If Kay could work her way through school, why couldn't he? Suddenly he was terribly ashamed of himself.
He had been thinking so much about school, and football, and feeling sorry for himself, that he hadn't given any thought at all as to how he might be able to help. What must his folks be thinking of him? They were so concerned about his going to school, were so willing to make any sacrifice, and he hadn't even offered to do what he could to help. He went into the house and sat down in the kitchen with his mother.
"You know," he said to her, "if I could just find a place where I could go to school, I know I could earn my room and board."
"Do you think so?" she asked doubtfully.
"Why, sure," he answered. "I got a letter from Kay

this morning. She's going to work for her board and room and go to school in Cedarton, Minnesota."

"She is?" Danny's mother echoed.

"Aunt Mabel wrote to them for her and made arrangements," Danny answered.

"Why, we've got some good friends in Cedarton," Mrs. Orlis exclaimed. "That's how the church there happened to take Mabel's support. They knew of her through your father and me."

Danny was silent a moment.

"Do you suppose," he began hesitantly, "that there'd be any chance of finding a place for me to board and room there so I could go to school, too?"

Mrs. Orlis dried her hands on the corner of her towel. "I don't know," she answered. "It could be. Although we haven't seen those folks for years and years."

"There must be quite a bunch of Christian kids in school there," he said, "with such a strong church and everything. Boy, it would really be great going to that school!"

"Of course, Kay wouldn't have anything to do with it being such a fine place to go to school, now would she?" his mother laughed.

The color came up in Danny's face to tint his cheeks delicately. "Not much," he grinned.

They talked it over that night and decided that Danny and his father should ride down to Warroad with Cap the next morning and get Tex to fly them to Cedarton.

"I don't know why we didn't think of Don Harms, and Felix and Edna Mullins, and some of the rest of those folk in Cedarton," Mr. Orlis said. "I'm certain that one of them would have a room we could rent for you, Danny."

"How come you know them so well?"

"Your mother and I lived in Cedarton for five years when we were first married," his dad said. "We were both baptized in the church there. We've got a lot of good friends around Cedarton."

Danny was so excited that night he could scarcely sleep. What he had said to Roxie a day or two before had been right after all. Things did work out according to God's will. Only he had to be ready and willing to do everything he could to help himself.

That had been the whole trouble before. He had been expecting his folks and God to do it all for him. Now he himself saw that he had to be willing to make sacrifices.

Impulsively he got up and knelt beside his bed.

"Lord Jesus," he prayed, "I do thank you for helping us to find a place where I might be able to go to school. I thank you, too, for helping me to see that I've got to do my part to help support myself. Help me to find a place to stay in Cedarton tomorrow. And if it is your will that I stay there, help me to find a job. Amen."

The next morning he and his dad went to Warroad by boat and flew to Cedarton where Mr. Orlis began looking up his old friends.

"I wish I could help you, Carl," Felix Mullins said when Mr. Orlis told him what he wanted, "but we're taking care of Edna's mother now. She's in the only spare bedroom we have."

"How about Don Harms?" Danny's dad asked. "Is he still around?"

"Don and Ruth moved to Florida last winter," he said "But I think you could find a room for Danny over at Mrs. Bill Barber's. Bill died this summer, and she's living over there all alone. She would probably like to get the extra money."

They got Danny a room with Mrs. Barber, and Tex and Mr. Orlis went back to Angle Inlet.

"Do you think you can get along now, Danny?"

"Sure thing, Dad. Mr. Mullins said he'd help me get a job if I wanted him to, and I can take care of registering."

His dad stuck out his hand and Danny took it and squeezed it hard. It was great to have a wonderful Christian dad.

Danny didn't even have his bag unpacked before the telephone rang, and Mrs. Barber called him to the phone.

"Say, Danny," the voice on the other end of the wire said, "this is Felix Mullins. I stopped in at the Ajax Station a few minutes ago. The manager said that he could use you washing cars and working at the gas pump after school and on Saturdays."

Danny was smiling broadly as he hung up. Just yesterday morning he had been up on the Angle worrying about whether he was going to be able to go to school or not. Now, here he was in Cedarton, with a place to stay and a job. It just showed how God worked.

School had already started in Cedarton, and he didn't want to lose any more time than he had already, so he washed and changed clothes and hurried over to the high school to register. The principal looked him over carefully.

"You look as though you've played a little football," Mr. Reimer said appraisingly.

"Yes, sir," Danny answered, "I have."

"What position?"

"Halfback at Iron Mountain," Danny went on. "We won the Colorado state championship last year."

"You did?" the principal echoed. "That's fine. We've got the possibilities of an outstanding team ourselves. Did you play regularly? I mean, were you in the starting lineup?"

"Yes, sir," Danny told him.

"Well now, that's something. We won our league championship last year, and have all the team back except two backfield men." He reached for the phone. "I'm going to call Coach Bennett and have him meet you. We can certainly use you."

Danny felt the sweat come out on his forehead. "I–I'm sorry," he said, "but I–I won't be able to play football this year."

Mr. Reimer stopped with his hand on the receiver. "You won't be able to play football?" he repeated.

"No, sir," Danny stammered. "I'm going to have to work in order to be able to go to school."

The principal straightened slowly. "I see," he said coldly.

FOUR
A tough decision

Danny stood there uneasily for a moment or two, staring at the principal.

"Miss Larsen will finish your registration," Mr. Reimer continued in that same icy tone. "I'm really very busy." With that he got up and strode brusquely out into the hall.

"What made him act like that?" Danny asked at last.

"Don't mind him," Miss Larsen said, smiling. "That football team is his pride and joy. When you told him that you were a regular halfback on the state championship team, he began to get visions of big things for Cedarton High."

A high school girl who was typing in the office looked up. "Mr. Reimer isn't the only one that the football team means a lot to," she said firmly. "It means a great deal to all of us."

Danny finished his registration and got out of the office as soon as he could. His face was burning. They acted as though he wouldn't be playing football because he didn't want to play, that he was afraid he would get hurt, or something. Didn't they understand that a guy might have to work to help pay his way through school? Didn't they know that he felt even worse than they did about not being able to go out for football?

One thing though, the Christian kids would understand. He could tell them how things were. They would know that he was doing what he had to do. And Kay! He smiled at the thought of her.

The final bell rang just then, and Danny stepped back into a doorway and waited. *There was just a chance that—* He stopped suddenly.

There she was, her arms full of books, and her soft blond hair blowing about her face. She was laughing and talking gayly to the girl beside her. Grinning, he stepped out into her path and waited. Just as he thought she would, she rammed into him, scattering her books across the floor.

"I beg your pardon," she exclaimed in embarrassment. "I–I didn't watch where I—" And then she recognized him. "Danny!" she cried. "Danny! Where have you been? What have you been doing? How come you're here?"

"Oh, I've been around," he grinned carelessly. "You never know where I'm going to show up."

"I certainly didn't expect to see you here," she said. "I thought by this time you'd be out in Colorado going to school."

"Changed my mind," he told her. "Or rather I had it changed for me."

"I've never been so surprised!" she said. "I've been hoping that I'd be able to get up to see your folks while I'm here, and that wonderful Angle country you talked about all the time, but I certainly didn't expect to see you."

"A couple of days ago I didn't expect to see you so soon, either," he told her. "Why don't we gather up these books and go some place where we can talk?"

They picked up the books and walked out of the school together.

"I'm so glad you're here, Danny," she said warmly. "Now I'll have one Christian friend here in school."

"There are a lot of Christian kids in Cedarton, aren't there?"

"I haven't found them yet."

"But the church is so big and active," he said. "I thought surely there would be a bunch of Christian kids about our age. That's been one of the things I've been looking forward to."

"So have I," she said. "But the high school class in Sunday school last Sunday was awfully small. There were only eight or ten kids in it. And I guess about the same bunch comes to Young People's."

They went into the corner ice cream shop and had a cold drink, making a little dent in Danny's already thin reserves. He had determined not to ask his dad for anything.

The two of them talked endlessly, of the trouble they had had in Mexico, and that frantic night when they had last seen one another.

"I was so frightened," Kay told him, "when you and Jim went off into the darkness with that manuscript down in Mexico. We stayed up all night long praying for you."

"The Lord got us safely through," he answered.

"The Indians, and all of us at the station, were so excited when we got your letter telling us all that had happened," she went on, "that we set aside a day of thanksgiving and prayer."

For a couple of minutes Danny sat there looking at her without saying anything. Kay was prettier than he had remembered her, with soft blond hair, and her complexion burned to a golden brown from being out in the hot Mexican sun. She was a great kid, and a great sport. He had never known anyone like her.

Kay looked up at the clock.

"Oh, Danny, I've got to run. I'm supposed to be home working at five o'clock, and it's five minutes to right now."

"How far do you have to go?" he asked, scooping up her books.

"It's only five or six blocks," she told him. "I stay with a woman who has four little youngsters, and help her for my room and board."

"Does she have a comfortable living room?" Danny asked. "I may be over to see you once in a while."

"You can come and help me baby-sit," she told him. "I'm supposed to get in on that on prayer meeting nights, and another night or two a week when there's something special going on at church, or she and her husband have to help with visitation."

"Sounds like a deal," he said. "Are you any good at algebra? I'll bring my lessons over for you to help me."

"I'm a whiz," she laughed.

The school at Cedarton wasn't as large as the one at Iron Mountain, but they had a fairly new building and a big gym. Danny really liked it better than the one at Colorado, except that the story of his football ability had spread like a forest fire throughout the school. And as it spread, it grew.

"Are you the new kid who was All-State for two years in Colorado?" one boy asked Danny the first morning he reported to his division room.

"We heard that you couldn't play because you've already signed up to play with the Chicago Bears as soon as you get out of high school," somebody else butted in.

"I'm afraid you're both wrong," Danny said, laughing. "Our team won the state championship last year in Colorado, but I didn't make All-State, and I'm not signed up with anybody to play ball."

"Then how come you're not going out for football here?" the guys demanded. "Boy, we need you! We lost both our halfback and quarter."

"I'm going to have to work," Danny tried to explain. "I won't have time for football."

The two boys turned away in disgust.

That night Danny hurried out of school just as the other guys were filing down into the locker room to change clothes. Two or three of them looked darkly at him and only grunted when he spoke. He stood there a moment or two, watching until they all disappeared down the stairs. It would sure be great to play again.

Down at the station, however, there wasn't time for him to think about football or anything else. There were three cars to wash, and he had to relieve the night man at the pumps for supper.

"We're going to put on another boy the first of next week," the manager told him. "But since I hired you first, you can choose the hours you want to work. You can work after school every afternoon, and all day Saturday, or you can work Saturday and Sunday. The hours are the same and the pay is the same."

"I think I'll work after school and Saturday," Danny said quickly, "if that's all right with you."

"Are you sure those are the hours you want, Danny?" his employer asked. "It will keep you from taking part in any sports. You can have the Sunday shift if you want it."

Danny shook his head. "I'll take the other one," he said.

"Well, if you want to change, you'll have to make up your mind right away," the manager retorted. "After we put on the other boy and he starts working one shift or the other, it'll be too late."

"Thanks," Danny answered, "but I know that this is what I want."

He had been so busy the first few days working and getting caught up with his class at school that he didn't get time to see Kay. But he called her from the station Thursday afternoon and took her to Young People's that evening.

"I've really got a problem," he said to her. "The coach and all the guys, and most of the kids at school it seems, are down on me for not going out for football."

"Don't they understand that you have to work for your board and room so that you can go to school?"

"I tried to tell them that, but they don't get it. They seem to think that I could go out for the team if I really wanted to."

"That's too bad," Kay said. "But they'll know after they get acquainted with you what the truth really is."

They had a good program at Young People's that

night, but Danny was the only boy, and there were only five girls besides Kay.

"We've just got to do something," she said as the two of them sat together on the front steps of the house where she stayed.

"If I could just get some of the guys interested," Danny said, "we would have a lot larger group. There ought to be quite a few who would like to come to our meetings if we could just find them."

"It's something we'll have to pray about," Kay told him.

"I wish you'd pray for me, too, Kay," he said seriously. "I'm not going to be able to do anything with the guys at school until I can make friends with them. And right now the whole bunch seem to have it in for me."

"Of course I will, Danny."

Before he left that evening, they bowed and prayed, asking God to help Danny make friends at school, and to help them get more guys and girls coming to Young People's.

The work at the station went well enough. Danny had never done anything like that before. But he soon learned to wash cars and do greasing and oil changes, in addition to working at the pumps. Mr. Cartwright raised his wages the first Saturday.

"I like the way you pitch in and do your share of the work, and a little more," he said.

"Thank you."

"The only thing I feel guilty about is giving you work that keeps you off the football team," he went on. "Mr. Reimer and Coach Bennett were in to see me this morning. They thought that perhaps you and I could work out some way so that you could be out for the team and still hold down your job. They realize that you're earning your way through school, and probably have your hands full."

"That would be fine," Danny acknowledged, "but I don't see how it can be done."

There was a moment's hesitation.

"You could take the Sunday shift you know," Mr. Cartwright suggested. "I could still make the switch so that you could be free after school."

Danny looked up at him. For a moment there was a longing inside.

"I would rather not," he said at last.

Mr. Cartwright sat down on the corner of his desk and eyed Danny quizzically.

"Would you mind telling me why not?"

"It—it's because I'm a Christian," Danny said. "I feel that I should take the shift that will give me the Lord's Day free."

The station manager picked up his pencil and studied it intently for a moment or two. "I have a big interest in our football team," he said slowly. "Always have. When I went to high school here, we won every game for two years straight." He stared at Danny. "Coach Bennett tells me that they called Iron Mountain and got a report that you were an outstanding Sophomore halfback, and showed real promise at quarter."

"I tried to play the best I could," Danny said.

"That's the way we got it," Cartwright went on. "That's why we've got to have you on that team. I've already promised the coach that you will be there."

Danny didn't say anything.

"I've hired another boy to work after school, Danny," his employer said. There was a tone of finality in his voice. "You will be working on Saturday and Sunday from now on."

FIVE
A costly choice

Danny stood there for a moment or two, as though he could scarcely understand what his employer meant.

"Do you mean that you want me to work the Sunday shift, Mr. Cartwright?" he asked.

"That's right, Danny," the station manager answered. "We want you to change shifts and go out on the football field and help give Cedarton the championship."

"But you told me that I could have my choice," Danny protested courteously. "You said that since I was the first one to go to work here that I could either take the afternoon shift during the week, or Sunday."

Mr. Cartwright pursed his lips.

"That was before I knew that you were a football player," he said bluntly. "I've always made it a practice to see that working here doesn't give any of the guys an excuse for missing out on football. Besides, I'd lose half my customers if they discovered that I had a star quarterback working down here instead of playing with the team. Football means a lot around this town, Danny. If you're going to get along here, you'd better remember that."

The telephone rang just then, and Mr. Cartwright was called out. Danny kept working, numbly. This was something that he hadn't counted upon.

That night after supper he went over to see Kay and told her what had happened.

"I don't know what to do," he told her. "I've got to have that job if I'm going to stay in school. And I really want to play football. I felt bad when I first found out that I wasn't going to be able to go back to Iron Mountain and play with the gang this fall. But I don't know about working on Sunday. I want to do what the Lord wants me to do, too. Dad certainly never worked on Sunday up at the Angle if he could possibly avoid it."

"Don't you think that Mr. Cartwright would let you take the afternoon shift if you insist on it?" she asked. "After all, he promised it to you."

Danny shook his head.

"I don't know," he answered. "He's quite a football fan. Why, he's still got pictures of himself in his football suit hanging in his private office. And the coach and principal came to him and asked him to work things out so that I'd be able to play."

"It's a big problem," she agreed.

"Of course," Danny went on, as though he scarcely heard her, "there are lots of jobs today where people have to work on Sunday. Take the railroad men and nurses and highway patrolmen, and the guys in the post office and hotels and cafes. They've all got to work on Sunday. If it's all right for them, I don't know why it isn't all right for me."

"Those are jobs that have to go on," Kay said. "A

real hardship would be worked on people everywhere if jobs like that weren't done. I believe that's different from washing cars."

"But I've got to go to school," he protested. "And if I do, I've got to have a job so I can earn my way."

"I know that, Danny," she told him. "I think the only thing we can do is to really pray about it and see what the Lord Jesus would have you do. That's the important thing: to be in the center of his will."

Danny walked slowly home that night and stood before the window in his room, looking out on the darkened street.

If Dad were just here so he could talk to him. If he could just ask him what he should do. But he couldn't. There wasn't anybody he knew well enough in Cedarton to go to for advice. This was something he would have to work out for himself. He knelt beside the bed and began to pray.

At the breakfast table the next morning, Mrs. Barber's twelve-year-old son Kirk said, "Well, Danny are you going out for football tonight?"

"I don't know," Danny answered. "I haven't decided yet."

"I sure hope you do," Kirk went on. "One of the guys said that Coach Bennett phoned the place where you went to school last year and found out that you were the best quarterback in the state."

"That's stretching it a little, I'm afraid," Danny said. "The fact is, I always considered myself a halfback."

He looked over at Kirk's sister, Karen, who was watching him wide-eyed, and smiled. She was a little older than Roxie, but she had that same sweet, elfin twist to her mouth and the same dancing dark eyes.

"If you go out for football, I'll yell for you, Danny," she assured him. "I'll yell like everything."

"If I should play, I'll certainly be listening for you, Karen," he said.

Danny went to school a little early that morning to finish studying his English. But as soon as he stepped inside the door, Butch Winston, the senior fullback, grabbed him.

"Say, Danny," Butch said, "Coach Bennett wants you to come up to his office right away."

"OK," he answered.

When he walked into the coach's office, he was surprised to see that Mr. Cartwright and the principal were there, too.

"Come in, sit down, Danny," the coach said pleasantly. "We'd like to talk with you for a few minutes."

He sat down nervously and looked from one to the other.

"I've told these gentlemen why you don't want to take Sunday work, Danny," Mr. Cartwright began. "And we all respect you for it. We want you to know that."

"That's right," the coach put in. "We've gone farther than that. I want you to know that I spent half of yesterday afternoon trying to locate a job for you that wouldn't require you to work on Sundays against your convictions."

"The truth of the matter is," Mr. Reimer said, "that there just aren't enough jobs available in a town the size of Cedarton."

"Don't you think that you could work on Sundays just during the football season?" Coach Bennett asked. "I'm sure that Mr. Cartwright would move you to the afternoon job when the season was over. Wouldn't you, John?"

"I'd sure try," his employer said.

There was a long silence. Danny could feel the eyes of the three men boring into him. He didn't intend to agree to take the Sunday shift, but somehow he couldn't bring himself to stand up against them.

"I—I—" he gulped hard. "I guess maybe I could."

"That's fine."

Coach Bennett got up and slapped him heartily on the back. Mr. Reimer and Mr. Cartwright shook his hand. "You'll not be sorry," his employer said. "I can assure you of that."

Word that Danny Orlis was going out for football set the school to buzzing. He could feel the change in the attitude of the guys as he went from class to class that day. They spoke to him in the hall, and five or six came up to talk to him.

"I believe I did the right thing," he said as he and Kay sat together in the lunchroom. "I don't believe I could ever have gotten next to any of those guys if I hadn't decided to go out for football. They wouldn't have had a thing to do with me. Now, maybe I can get some of them to come to Young People's."

"I hope things work out all right, Danny," she said.

"What's the matter?" he asked quickly. "Don't you think I decided right?"

"I don't know," she answered. "I was wondering about your testimony with them, even if you do make friends. What will they think of Jesus and your love for him, if you're working on his day so that you can play football?"

Danny sat there for a long while, chewing thoughtfully on his lower lip. Kay's soft, probing question bothered him all the rest of the afternoon in class. It bothered him as he checked out a football suit and went out onto the field. But the warm, friendly way the coach and the guys on the team treated him soon dulled the hurt in his heart.

Coach Bennett gave him the list of signals to memorize, and put him to playing quarter, with one of the other guys calling the signals from the halfback position. Danny soon saw that the coach and Mr. Cartwright hadn't been mistaken when they had said Cedarton was going to have a good football team. The guys were big and hard and fast, and had the advantage over him of having been in practice for a month.

"How's it going, Danny?" Coach Bennett asked.

"All right, I guess," he answered uncertainly. "I don't know why, but I feel so awkward and clumsy out there."

"Just keep plugging away," the coach told him. "You're a little out of condition now, and the rest of the squad has a game under their belt. You'll come along OK, I'm sure of that. And you're going to be a lot of help to us when you are ready."

Back at Mrs. Barber's that night, Kirk and Karen were jubilant when they heard the news.

"You went out for the team today, didn't you, Danny?" Kirk said. "I rode by on my bike and saw you. Boy, was I glad! With you out there, we've got that championship in the bag."

"I don't think I'll make that much difference," Danny said. "The fact is, as good a squad as we've got here, I might not even make the starting eleven."

"Don't kid me," Kirk said loyally. "I know what kind of a player you were back in Colorado."

"It looks as though you've got a couple of real fans, Danny," Hannah Barber said, coming into the kitchen. "All they've been able to talk about is you and whether you were going to go out for the team. I'm surely glad that you decided the way you did. I don't know whether they could have stood it if you hadn't chosen to play football."

"I love to play," Danny told her. "The only thing that bothers me is working on Sunday. I had to change to the Sunday shift at the station in order to have the afternoons free to practice."

She looked at him quizzically. "Why should that make any difference?" she asked.

"It's the Lord's Day," he told her. "I know there are a lot of jobs that are a public service and have to be kept going, but people can get their cars washed and greased any time. I had quite a problem deciding whether it was right for me to work on Sunday or not."

"I never heard of such a thing," the graying young widow said. "Sunday isn't any different from any other day."

"Don't you and Karen and Kirk go to church on Sunday?" Danny asked.

She shook her head.

For an instant or two he sat there. Somehow he had supposed that most people went to church on Sunday.

He turned to Kirk. "You'd like to go to Sunday school, wouldn't you, fella?"

Kirk eyed him suspiciously.

"Do you go?" Kirk asked him.

"Sure I do. Every Sunday."

"Then I'll go with you."

"And so will I," his sister put in.

"You don't care, do you?" he asked their mother.

"It doesn't make any difference to me," Mrs. Barber said wearily. "I suppose they'll be as well off there as they would be on the street, or at home reading the Sunday funnies."

"You'll go with us, won't you?" Kirk asked Danny again.

"Certainly I will. I—" he stopped short. "I almost forgot. I'll be working that day, but I'll have Kay Milburn stop by for you. She'll take you with her."

"Nothing doing!" Kirk said firmly. "I'm not going with any girl!"

A sharp, stabbing pain shot into his heart.

It lay there all night, and was still with him the following day and into the evening as he dressed for his first football game.

Neither Kirk nor Karen was a Christian. They would go to church and Sunday school with him, but Kirk could never go with a girl. That would be "sissy", as far as he was concerned. Instead of being able to take them to Sunday school where they would hear about the Lord Jesus, Danny was going to be working, desecrating the Lord's Day.

On the first play, Ken Albert called his signal, but Danny was thinking about Kirk and fumbled. Wharton recovered and two plays later crossed the Cedarton goal line.

"Orlis!" Coach Bennett shouted angrily. "Wake up out there!"

SIX
A nagging ache

When Danny reported for work Saturday morning, Mr. Cartwright called him into his office.

"What was the trouble last night, Danny?" he asked. "You didn't get going so well."

"I know it," he admitted. "I haven't been playing like the other guys have, and I'm a little out of condition."

"You want to get in condition and get in there and dig," his employer told him. "It means something to win those ball games. It means a lot. We almost lost on your account last night."

"I'll do my best," he said.

"I know you will."

There was a great deal of work to do at the station that day, and it was after six o'clock when Danny washed and greased the last car and checked out.

"You'll be down in the morning, won't you?" his employer reminded him.

Danny nodded. "About eight o'clock?"

"That's right. Joe will be here early, but I won't be

around until nine or ten. I usually sleep late on Sunday morning."

Danny talked with Karen and Kirk when he got home, asking them again to go to Sunday school with Kay the following morning.

"I'm going," Karen said, "but Kirk won't."

"I wouldn't mind going," Kirk maintained stoutly, "but I don't want to go in there with a couple of girls."

"There'll be a lot of guys at Sunday school, Kirk," Danny told him. "Almost as many boys as there are girls. And you'll be in a great class."

"Will you be there?" he asked.

Danny shook his head reluctantly.

"Will any of the football team be there?"

"It doesn't make any difference who's in the congregation," Danny said quietly. "We know that Jesus will be there. That's the main thing."

"If you were going, I might think about it." Danny looked away. If only he didn't have to work in the morning!

That night he tossed and turned sleeplessly. He prayed, but somehow there wasn't the peace and satisfaction that usually came.

Sunday morning he called Kay from the station to be sure that she was going by to pick up Karen.

All day long he was miserable. Nothing seemed to go right. The owner of the first car he greased came back in twenty minutes and bawled him out for not oiling the door hinges. About the time Sunday school would have started, a woman brought her car in to be washed, and stood there, tapping her foot impatiently, until he finally got it finished. And during the noon hour he was so flustered he gave a stranger ten dollars in change for a five and had to run after him to get it back.

"I never put in such a day, Kay," he said as they walked down the street toward her place. "It didn't seem like Sunday at all, and nothing went right for me."

Kay nodded understandingly. "I've had days like that."

"How did Karen like Sunday school?"

"She loved it. I don't believe she had ever been there before, from the way she acted. She didn't know anything about Christ or the disciples or anything. She sat wide-eyed all through the service, and on the way home asked me all sorts of questions."

He smiled. "I guess that's one good thing that happened today," he said.

"I wish Kirk would have come, too," she continued. "He was in his old clothes playing ball outside when we got home."

Danny nodded and changed the subject quickly.

Monday evening on the football field, Coach Bennett took Danny off to one side and worked with him alone for half an hour or so, showing him the way he wanted him to stand and fake on the plays.

"We've got a big job teaching you our style of play, all our plays, and getting you into condition, too, Danny," he said. "We won't be able to do it unless you give us everything you've got. In addition to our regular practices, I'm going to ask you to put in half an hour or more on the track, running. You've got to get in shape."

Danny was getting into condition rapidly. He didn't smoke like some of the guys did or eat a lot of candy.

And he had worked hard up at the Angle. It didn't take much to put him in condition.

But playing was something else again. They used several formations that were new to him, and handled the ball differently from the way he had been taught at Iron Mountain. He was tense and over-anxious during scrimmage, and the dull aching pain of his working on the Lord's Day gnawed like a canker at his heart.

They scrimmaged on Wednesday night, and Danny began to find himself. He broke away for two long runs and rifled a pass that was good for a touchdown against the second team.

"Just keep that up, Danny," Coach Bennett said. "You're getting back in the groove now."

Danny grinned happily. It was coming back to him now. He could feel it. He was getting confidence in himself in handling a football again. The old thrill came back.

Thursday afternoon they had a light practice which ended early, and Danny was able to get to Young People's on time. Kay and another girl were sitting on the front step of the dark church.

"What's the trouble?" he asked.

"No one told the janitor we'd be meeting tonight," Kay said, "and the church is locked."

"That's too bad. How long have you been here?"

"Oh, we just came," the other girl put in. "Karen and Debbie went for the key."

"We don't know how many kids came early for Young People's," Danny said. "Has this happened very often?"

"The church was locked one other time since I've

been coming to Young People's," Kay said.

"Oh, it's happened lots of times," Lori Shively said. "You see, we change our meeting night around a lot, or postpone it for basketball games and special meetings in some of the country churches or things like that. Sometimes the janitor gets mixed up and opens the church when we aren't going to meet or leaves it locked when we are."

Danny and the four girls who had come to church together were all that were present at Young People's that night. The meeting fell flat, and they sat around for an hour or so after it was over, talking about their group and what they could do to get it to moving again.

"We've got to do something or we'd just as well quit," Lori said. "We can't go on like this. We aren't doing the church, or ourselves, or anyone else any good."

"You're right about that," Danny observed. "There aren't even enough of us to have a good meeting."

"But what can we do?" Kay asked.

Danny shook his head.

After they left the church, he and Kay walked down to the ice cream shop for a malt and talked about it some more, but there didn't seem to be any answers.

"There are a lot of older folk in the church," Kay said, "but there doesn't seem to be many kids, even in Sunday school. I don't think I ever saw a church like it."

"If we just had a few guys as well as girls coming regularly, we might be able to get something done."

"We'll have to pray about it some more, Danny," she told him, getting to her feet and slipping into her jacket.

The next evening on the football field all went well

for Danny. It was one of those nights when everything that he did was right. By this time he had learned the signals and was calling the plays from his position at quarter.

On the first day he flipped a short shovel pass over the line, and Eddie Chambers tucked it in and scampered for the goal line. Midway in the second quarter, he scored a touchdown himself on a long twisting run. The game ended 27 to 6 and the Cedarton fans went wild. Edgar City had been picked to beat them easily by both the Minneapolis and St. Paul papers.

"Danny Orlis was the difference," the local daily boasted Saturday afternoon, "as he ran and passed and guided the Cedarton Eagles to a stunning, although unexpected, victory. If he can go against Brighton and Willow Creek with the same cool-headed speed and ability, Cedarton should be able to coast undefeated through the rest of their schedule. . . ."

There was more, but Danny didn't read it. He always felt a little foolish when he saw things like that in the paper about himself. For he knew that it was just one of those good nights and that his teammates deserved most of the credit for the support they gave him.

Down at the station Sunday morning he felt the same way that he did the week before. That same nagging ache lay like a ball of ice in the pit of his stomach.

He washed the only car that was there, swept out the station, and put the tools away. He was standing in the doorway when a little guy about Kirk's age came riding up on his bicycle.

"Say, Joey," he said, "don't you belong to our Sunday school?"
"Yep," Joey replied. "Give me a package of gum."
Danny went inside and got the gum.
"Say," the younger lad said, admiringly, "that was some game you played Friday night! Boy, were you hot!"
"How come you aren't in Sunday school today?" Danny asked.
"I don't know," Joey mumbled, taking a stick of gum out of the package.
"Oh, yes, you do," Danny persisted. "Come on now, what's the reason?"
Joey offered him a stick of gum.
"Mom wanted me to go," he said, "but I told her that you didn't go to Sunday school anymore, and neither am I!"
The words stuck like a knife in Danny's heart!
So that was what his testimony was doing!

SEVEN
Unknown future

Danny stood in the doorway of the station and watched Joey pedal happily down the street. If he had been in Sunday school himself, Joey would have been there too. And so would Kirk. His landlady's son wouldn't go to Sunday school with Kay and his sister, but he would have gone with him.

That was what his testimony was doing in Cedarton! And he had hoped to win some of the guys to Christ! He ran his fingers through his tousled sandy hair and turned miserably back to the grease rack.

"Hey, Danny," Mr. Cartwright called from the pumps. "Would you fill my car with gas?"

"Sure thing." Danny laid down his gloves and started toward the car.

"I'll take care of it, Mr. Cartwright," the regular attendant said.

"Never mind," he told him, "I want to talk to Danny."

Danny took off the gas cap of his employer's big car and started to put in the gas.

"We mowed 'em down Friday night, didn't we, Danny boy?" he said. "We really mowed 'em down."

"We did have a good night," Danny agreed. "All the guys were going good."

"The guys were going good because you sparked them, Orlis," the station manager said. "I've seen those kids play before. It takes a real quarterback to get them to go the way they were going Friday night."

Danny said nothing.

"You keep going like you did Friday," he continued, "and you're likely to find yourself with a nice raise."

Danny looked at him quizzically.

"I cleaned up a hundred bucks on that game Friday night," his employer went on. "Now I'm going over to Brighton and try to pick up some bets before the papers get over there with the story of how we slaughtered Wharton. They think that they've got a good team, but we'll show 'em. We'll show 'em."

Danny stood beside the pump watching Mr. Cartwright's car until it disappeared onto the highway.

"Everything's OK for you now, Orlis," the pump attendant laughed good-naturedly. "But wait until you call a bum play, or fumble and cost him a hundred or so. We'll have to hide you somewhere until he cools down."

"So that's why he's so interested in football," Danny said. "Does everybody here in Cedarton bet on the games? Is that why they have such good crowds?"

"Oh, no," his fellow worker answered. "I don't suppose that there are half a dozen guys who bet that much. But they're the ones who can't bear to lose. They feel like they've got to go in and help the coach all they can, and even try to get new players. And when the coach loses, they begin to howl for a new one. The rest of us just go out to see a good game."

That evening Kay stopped by on the way home from church and waited until he got off work.

"Well," she said, "how did it go today, Danny?"

"Terrible," he told her. "I don't believe that I ever put in such a miserable day."

"What went wrong?"

"It's this Sunday-working business," be blurted. He told her about Joey coming down to the station during Sunday school. "Kirk was the same way," he went on. "And the worst of it is that there isn't a single thing I can do about it. I've got to have that job or I can't go to school."

Kay was silent for a long while. "Do you really believe that, Danny?" she asked.

"Why?" he countered quickly. "What do you mean?"

"I don't know whether I can say it just the way I want to or not," she went on, "but I was just thinking that if you're convinced in your own mind that you shouldn't work on Sunday, and if you really prayed about it and put your trust in God, he would help you to find another job."

"But I've tried," he replied. "I've been praying about it ever since I got here, and Coach Bennett went all over town looking for a job for me that didn't involve working on Sunday. He couldn't find a thing."

"You weren't putting your trust in Jesus that way though," Kay went on. "You still had this job, and you were praying for another one to take its place. We found out on the mission field that if we are actually going to put our trust in Christ, we have to do what we know is right and depend upon him to take care of us. We can't wait to see how it all is going to turn out first."

"But I've got to pay Mrs. Barber regularly," he said. "And I've got to have money for lunch at school and a few supplies."

"Mother always said that it was times like this that really proved how much we trust and believe God when he tells us that he will answer our prayers."

Danny went to bed at the usual time that night, but he couldn't sleep. There were a lot of people who had to work on Sunday, he told himself doggedly. No one thought anything about it at all. Why should it make so much difference whether he worked or not? And what would he do if he did quit? Mrs. Barber didn't have money enough to give him credit for over a week or two on his board and room. All she had was a little magazine subscription business to support herself and the children.

He got up and sat on the side of the bed. Questions were spinning in his mind. But he couldn't forget Joey or Kirk. If they didn't go to Sunday school because he didn't, then he was responsible. He sighed deeply and crawled back into bed and tried to pray. He knew then what he had to do.

"Lord Jesus," he prayed, "I know I can't work at the station any longer. I've got to quit football and find a job that won't make me work on Sunday. Please help me, O Lord. I–I'm putting my trust in thee."

The next morning he left home a little early and stopped at the station to tell Mr. Cartwright that he wouldn't be able to work for him anymore.

"What's that going to do to your football playing?" the station owner demanded.

"I'm going to have to quit," Danny told him, "and get a week-day job."

Mr. Cartwright sat at his desk for a moment, staring at the floor.

"I don't feel that I can work on Sunday," Danny went on. "It was a hard thing to decide, but I made it a real matter of prayer, and I know that God would have me work during the week instead."

"A religious fanatic," the station manager snorted.

When Danny got to school, Coach Bennett was waiting for him at the front door.

"Mr. Cartwright called me a few minutes ago, Danny," he said. "I'd like to talk to you for a minute. Is what he said true?"

Danny nodded.

"A lot of good Christians work on Sunday."

"I know that. I feel that it's something a guy has to decide for himself. I thought it was all right. Or rather, I tried to make myself believe that it was all right for me to work on Sunday, but I found that some of the younger kids were staying away from Sunday school because I did."

"I don't see what that's got to do with it."

"The Bible tells us that if we're doing something that's causing someone else trouble, we had better stop what we're doing," Danny tried to explain.

"If that's the way things are, I suppose there's no use in talking," he said. "But I want you to know this: I think you're letting me down and the team and the school down by doing what you're doing. What do you think the football gang is going to think of your precious religion when they find out that you've quit them flat when you could help win the state championship?"

Danny didn't speak. He couldn't. His throat choked, and his mouth went hot and dry. Finally, he turned and walked hesitantly down the corridor to his division room.

That night after school he went down to the locker room and checked in his equipment to the student manager. The guys all eyed him, but nobody spoke or acted as though they even knew him. Coach Bennett came in, grim and tight-lipped.

"All right, guys," he said, looking straight at Danny. "Let's get out on the field."

Danny went downtown that afternoon and began to go from one store to another, but the answer was always the same. The grocery stores had their delivery boys. The ice cream store used girls at their soda fountain. The filling stations wanted guys who would work on Sunday.

"I don't know what to do, Kay," he said dejectedly that night. "I've just about made the rounds, but I can't find any work."

"You don't want to get discouraged," she told him. "The important thing is to be in God's will. If we're sure of that, everything else will work out."

"But I'm not sure of that," he said. "We've been concerned about the Young People's Society at church and have been wanting to get it going. But how am I going to influence any of the guys to come now? My name's poison around school."

"I knew a girl one time who tried to win her boyfriend to Christ by going to parties with him so that he'd go to church with her," she said. "But it never works out that way. I don't think God uses things like that to work for good."

"I don't believe I follow you, Kay," he said. "Just what do you mean?"

"Well," she replied. "I don't think you could ever win the guys to Christ by working on Sunday against your convictions so that you could play football with them."

"I wish I could be sure that you're right," he said doubtfully.

EIGHT
A new job

In a way Danny felt relieved that he wasn't working at the station on Sunday anymore. The quick stab of pain as he walked past the place, or saw Kirk and Joey was gone. Yet his problems seemed bigger than ever. By Tuesday morning the whole school knew that he wasn't playing football anymore. And, just as Coach Bennett had said, the kids were furious.

"You can't tell me he's that religious," Rick Haines said as he and one of the other guys went out of history class ahead of Danny. "I'll bet he got mad at the coach or something."

"He got hit pretty hard a couple of times," the other replied. "Maybe he just can't take it. That kind of a guy usually can't."

"He's not such a hot player, anyhow," Rick continued. "He was just lucky Friday night."

Danny's ears burned as he walked along behind them to the next classroom.

Rick turned enough to see him.

"Anyhow," he said, even louder than before, "Orlis is

done here at Cedarton. If he doesn't have any more school spirit than that, we don't want him on the team. We'll win our games without him."

"That's what I say."

So that was what they thought of him. How could he ever win any of them to Christ when they felt that way? How could he even make any friends here in Cedarton? It wasn't like that back home on the Angle. They knew him there. Suddenly he was terribly homesick.

Danny went out that afternoon as soon as school was out and again tried to find a job, but it was the same story.

"I couldn't hire you, even if I wanted to," one businessman told him. "I make it a practice not to hire high school guys during the football or hockey season. You guys should be out for the team."

"But I've got to work," Danny protested, "if I'm going to stay in school."

The man looked at him queerly. "I understand you had a good job and quit it for some foolish notion."

When Danny got home that night, Mrs. Barber was sitting in the living room, mending some of Kirk's socks.

"I wish I could help you, Danny," she said seriously, "but I've got all that I can do to keep my family fed and clothed."

"I know that," he told her. "I've got money enough to pay my board and room for another week. I'm trusting in the Lord to take care of me from then on."

"You really believe that, don't you?" she said doubtfully.

"Of course I do."

"When you get as old as I am, you'll know better."
"Dad and Mother are older than you," he replied, "and they put their trust in Jesus."
"But they've never had the hard knocks I've had," she went on. "All I've got to support myself and the youngsters is what I get from your room and my little magazine subscription business."
The phone rang just then, and she went to answer it. "It was for you, Danny," she said a moment later. "Kay called and asked me to tell you that the committee meeting is at the church tonight at 7:30."
The committee meeting turned out to be just about like a regular Young People's meeting. The same three girls met with Kay and Danny.
"I guess we all know what this is about," Lori, who was the president, said. "Kay and I thought that we had better meet tonight and see if we can figure out something we can do about our society. Does anyone have any suggestions?"
There was a long silence.
"How about you, Cathy?"
She shook her head.
"I don't know, unless we could get some of the guys out. If they'd come, we could easily get some more girls."
"I'd sort of been hoping that Danny would be able to get some of them to come," Lori said, "but I don't suppose that would work now."
He felt the color drain out of his cheeks.
"Maybe we could get some outstanding programs," she continued.
"That sounds good to me," Cathy put in quickly.
The idea sounded good to Danny on the surface, but Kay was hesitant.

"I keep wondering," she said, "what would happen to our society when we quit having special attractions. We couldn't keep that up for very long. I'm afraid when we did have to stop, we'd lose all our crowd."

"Well," Lori asked petulantly, "what would you do?"

"I've been thinking and praying a lot about this," Kay said earnestly. "My idea won't sound very exciting, but it does work on the mission field."

"Well, come on," Danny laughed, "out with it."

"It's really so simple that it doesn't sound like anything at all," Kay went on, "but each one of us ought to pick out some certain guy or girl we want to get to come to Young People's and start praying for him. Then when we've really pleaded with the Lord to help us to get him to come, we ought to start asking him."

"What if he doesn't come then?"

"Keep on praying for him and asking him until he does."

"I think you really hit on something," Danny told Kay when the meeting was over and they were walking home together. "But it'll never work with me. I can't get any of the guys to come, the way they feel about me."

"Where's your faith, Danny?" she asked.

He shook his head dismally.

Danny hadn't intended going to the football game Friday night, but Kay didn't have anyone to go with, so he went along with her.

"I feel like a monkey being on the sidelines," he told her self-consciously. "Do you know that I've never watched a football game from the stands before?"

"We can yell, anyway," she laughed.

"I would, if I were you," a voice behind them said coldly.

Danny turned. There sat Mr. Cartwright, staring bleakly at him.

The first half was a hard seesaw battle with Cedarton leading by a single point, but the third quarter was tragic. The Cedarton signal caller muffed two plays in a row, then in desperation called Danny's favorite pass play and rifled the ball directly into the arms of a Brighton man. He scored standing up.

"Well, Orlis," Mr. Cartwright said, "are you satisfied?"

In a matter of minutes Brighton scored again, and then Cedarton settled down to hold them. When the game was finally over, Danny and Kay allowed themselves to be shoved along with the crowd until they reached the gate.

"I was hoping they'd win tonight," he said at last. "It would surely have taken a lot of the pressure off me."

"Do you know what Mother always says about that?" Kay asked. "She says that God didn't promise to make things easy for any of us. He only promised to give us the strength and courage we need to overcome the trouble that does come our way."

"I guess your mother's right at that," he said. "But I've been praying and praying so much lately without any answers, that I've become terribly discouraged."

"Things will work out, Danny," Kay said confidently. The next morning when he came down for breakfast, he paid Mrs. Barber for the week's board and room.

"Are you sure you can spare this, Danny?"

"I can spare it this week," he said. "I don't know about next week."

"Have you got any work?"

"Nope."

Mrs. Barber poured him a glass of milk.

"I've just been thinking," she said. "I've got this magazine and newspaper subscription business, but I'm not able to take care of it like I should. Do you think you could help me with it?"

"I don't know," he said. "In what way?"

"I need someone who has the time to go out and make calls, and address circulars and envelopes to prospective customers," she went on. "I couldn't afford to pay you any definite wages. It would have to be on a commission basis, but if you'd like to try it, I'd like to see what you can do."

"Would I?" he exclaimed jubilantly. "Just give me a chance.

While they were still sitting at the table talking over plans for the job, Kirk came in quietly and started upstairs.

"Kirk," his mother said, "what on earth's the matter with you?"

"Nothing," he said shortly. "Why?"

"Look at your clothes!" she exclaimed. "And your face! Kirk, you've been in a fight!"

He wiped at the dirt on his cheeks.

"You know I don't allow you to fight. What was it about this time?"

"That—that Don Haines," Kirk began, his voice still trembling, "he said that Danny was a coward and a bunch of other stuff. And he wouldn't take it back, until I made him!"

“You weren’t fighting over me, were you, Kirk?” Danny demanded.

“He—he said that everybody in town was talking about you,” Kirk went on, “especially since the game last night!”

NINE
What next?

"You weren't fighting about me, were you, Kirk?" Danny repeated quickly.

"He can't call you names in front of me and get away with it," Kirk went on defiantly. "I don't care if you're not playing football."

"You shouldn't do that," his mother scolded. "I don't want you fighting over Danny or anything else."

Danny went over to where the younger boy was sitting and looped his arm across his shoulder.

"Listen, fella," he began softly. "I appreciate your sticking up for me and all that, but fighting doesn't solve anything."

"He said some awful things about you," Kirk protested.

"That's all right," Danny went on. "It still isn't anything to fight about. When Jesus was here on earth, people mocked him and beat him and then made him carry a heavy cross up a hill where they crucified him on it. He was God. All he had to do was to speak, and a whole host of angels would have killed every one of them. But he didn't. He died on the cross and rose again to save us from sin."

"Is that true, Danny?"

"It tells all about it in the Bible, Kirk," he answered. "And the Bible is the Word of God."

Kirk chewed on his lower lip.

"Don't you think we ought to go over and apologize to Don?" Danny suggested quietly.

For a moment or two Kirk didn't move. Finally he turned to Danny. "Would you go over with me if I do?" he asked.

"Sure thing."

"You'd better wash the dirt from your face first," his mother said. She looked up at Danny when Kirk was gone, as though she was about to speak. Then she stopped and dropped her gaze quickly. He saw that her tired brown eyes were brimming with tears.

"We'll be back in a little while, Mrs. Barber."

It wasn't far to Don Haines' house where he lived with his parents and older brother Rick. Don was out in the yard working on his bicycle when they came up.

"What are you doing here?" he demanded angrily. "Why'd you come over here?"

"We want to talk to you a couple of minutes," Danny said pleasantly.

"Well, I don't want to talk to you."

Just then Rick came out of the house. "What's the matter, Don? Are they giving you a bad time?"

"I'm not going to take back what I said," Don snapped. "I don't care if you did bring Danny over here to try and make me. I think he's a chicken and a poor sport, and a—a religious fanatic. And nobody at school has any use for him."

"That goes double," Rick put in.

Danny felt the color climb to his cheeks, but he fought to control himself. "We came over because Kirk has something he wants to tell you, Don," Danny replied.

Kirk Barber stood there biting his lower lip. "I–I came over to tell you that I–I'm sorry for fighting with you, Don," he blurted.

Don stared at him.

"I shouldn't have plowed into you the way I did." He held out his hand clumsily.

For an instant the other boy stared at him as though he didn't know what to do. Then he took Kirk's hand in his own. "I–I guess I shouldn't have said what I did, either, Kirk," he replied haltingly.

They looked at each other and grinned.

"How about helping me fix my bike, Kirk?" Don asked. "You always were the best guy in the neighborhood on coaster brakes."

Together they squatted beside the bike and went to work.

"Thanks, Danny," Rick said slowly. "These two guys have always been the best of pals. We sure don't want them fighting each other."

"That's right."

With that Rick turned and went into the house, leaving Danny standing there.

That afternoon he gathered up a few sample magazines and some subscription blanks and began to make the rounds of the houses in the neighborhood. He had never done any selling, but he rather liked it. And surprisingly enough, he was able to make a few sales. When he got back to the house and added up his commission, he discovered that he had earned more than he would have made by working all day at the filling station.

"And I'm just getting started," he told Kay jubilantly that night. "I hardly know anything about the magazines yet. But I'm getting some prospects lined up. And another thing, I'm planning to get some good Christian magazines on the list, too."

"Do you remember what we were talking about the other night?" she asked.

"About how the Lord will take care of us if we put our trust in him?" he finished.

"Now you've got a better job and are making more money than you did when you were working at the station. And besides, you're helping Mrs. Barber. Every time you sell a subscription you're helping her take care of Kirk and Karen."

"I'd never thought of that," Danny said.

"It's wonderful to be a Christian and know that God is watching over us and helping us according to his will," Kay said.

Danny nodded.

"That's why I know that if we all pray for our Young People's Society and pray for certain kids to come, that we'll be able to build it up to what it ought to be.

He was quiet for a minute or two.

"You know," he said at last, "I've got a little confession to make. I've been so concerned about my own problems that I haven't been praying for anyone to come to Young People's."

"It isn't too late to start."

"I've got a guy picked out whom I'm going to pray for though," Danny said. "Rick Haines."

"That's strange," Kay replied. "I picked Marilyn Forester. He goes with her, doesn't he?"

"I think so."

The next morning when Danny came down for breakfast, Kirk was sitting in the living room putting on his shoes.

"Well, are you going to Sunday school this morning?" Danny asked him.

Kirk looked up questioningly. "Are you going?"

"Sure thing."

"Would you take Don, too?" the younger boy asked.

"Of course," Danny said.

Kirk went into the other room, and Danny sat down to study his Sunday school lesson. In a few minutes the younger boy was back.

"He can't go. I don't think I will either."

"Now listen," Danny told him, "you can't let me down like that. Come on and get your good clothes on."

"I'll go with you next Sunday."

"Come on," Danny urged. "You can go with me next Sunday, too."

They walked over to the church together and Danny introduced Kirk to Ted Bailey, his Sunday school teacher.

Ted had one of the boys read the lesson from the Bible and then asked different ones to explain what had been read. It was surprising to Kirk how much some of the boys knew about the Bible. He didn't know anything. And when Ted asked him a question, he got red and flustered and had to mutter that he didn't know. But none of the guys laughed.

Then toward the close of the period, Ted sort of

summed up everything that had been said and gave a little talk about sin. That was what floored Kirk. He had never heard anything like that before. Once or twice he almost raised his hand to ask a question, but he didn't. He couldn't let the guys know how ignorant he was, nor how that icy pain that had come as Ted talked about the consequences of sin lay in his heart without melting.

"Well, Kirk," Danny said when Sunday school was over, "how about staying for church?"

"OK," he said quickly.

Danny went to church again that night. It was 9:30 when he got back home. The house was dark except for a light in Kirk's room.

"That's strange," Danny said to himself as he went into the house. "Usually the Barbers all go out together."

He picked up his books from the library table and started upstairs. In front of Kirk's room he stopped suddenly and listened.

The door was open, and the sound of deep, agonizing sobs came from within. Danny's heart leaped to his throat! Kirk! Something was wrong with him!

TEN
The light dawns

Danny stood there beside Kirk's door, listening. The younger boy was lying across the bed, sobbing pitifully. His heart faltered a little. There must be something terribly wrong.

"What's the matter, Kirk?" he asked, opening the door.

Kirk didn't act as though he had heard him. "Kirk," Danny said, grasping him by the shoulder and shaking him gently. "What happened?"

After a moment or two the younger boy turned slowly and sat up, wiping at his eyes. "There's nothing wrong," he managed.

Danny sat down on the bed beside him. "I know better."

"Mother and Karen went to a show tonight," he stammered.

"That's not what you're crying about." Danny said.

Kirk was still wiping his eyes with the back of his

grimy hand. "You won't laugh at me, will you?" he asked.

"Of course not."

"Are you positive?"

"Positive."

"Well," Kirk began hesitantly, "I listened to what Ted Bailey had to say about sin and Christ and things like that. And then the preacher talked about them, too. I—I—" he stopped for an instant and gulped hard.

Danny nodded sympathetically, but said nothing.

"I never have felt so terrible in my life," the boy went on. "I decided to stay at home and read the Bible Ted lent me. He marked some places for me to read, but it didn't help a bit."

"What do you mean, it didn't help?" Danny asked.

"It made me feel all the worse," Kirk continued. "Danny, I'm lost. It says so in the Bible, in those verses that Ted marked for me. If—if I died tonight, I wouldn't go to heaven."

Danny reached over and got the Bible. "But you *can* go to heaven, Kirk," he said softly, "if you really want to."

A smile broke through on Kirk's face.

"All you have to do is—"

Danny stopped. Last year he had led Larry to Christ, but this was different. He had to be sure to make his explanation simple enough for Kirk to understand. He had to be able to explain God's plan of salvation so the boy, who knew little or nothing of the gospel, could grasp it. Hurriedly he thumbed through the Bible, looking for some Scripture that would help, but at the moment he could find none.

"Just a minute," he said to Kirk. "I'm going to call someone."

Pastor Carlstrom wasn't home and wouldn't be back for an hour or more, so Danny called Kay.

"I'll be there in ten minutes," she said.

Danny and Kirk were sitting in the living room reading the verses Ted had marked when she knocked at the door.

"It's really very simple, Kirk," she said as she opened her Bible. "You already understand that 'all have sinned,' and that includes you. That's the most important thing."

Kirk smiled weakly.

"Before anyone can be saved," she went on, "he has to realize that he is a sinner and needs a Savior. Then he has to put his trust in Jesus to save him from sin."

"How do you do that?"

"Do you believe the Bible when it says that Christ came into the world to save sinners?"

"Yes," he answered.

"Do you believe that he can save you from sin?"

He nodded, his lower lip trembling again.

"Are you ready to put your trust in him?" she asked. "Are you ready to say, 'Lord, I know that I'm a sinner and deserve to be lost, but I have faith that Jesus can save me from sin. I'm going to put my trust in him for salvation, and with his help I'm going to live the way he wants me to live'? Can you pray that way and really and truly mean it?"

"I–I think so."

Together the three of them knelt and prayed as Kirk asked Jesus to be his Savior.

Danny had some studying to do that night, but now all thoughts of it were gone. He and Kay and Kirk sat in the living room and talked until Karen and her mother came home.

"You'd better run up to bed now, Kirk," Mrs. Barber said as she came into the room where they were sitting.

"OK, Mother." He got up quickly.

"Now what got into him?" Mrs. Barber asked aloud. "Usually I have to drag him up to bed."

Danny did not answer.

"Why didn't you tell Kirk's mother what happened?" Kay asked as they walked down the tree-lined street toward her house.

"I thought he should be the first to tell her." That night Danny prayed longer and harder than he had ever prayed before for Rick Haines and Kirk.

The next few days after school he worked hard selling subscriptions. Mrs. Barber was jubilant at the success that he had.

"I don't know how you do it, Danny," she said when they added his sales for the first week, "but you've sold more in a week than I usually sell in a month."

"I pray a lot about it."

Her face clouded queerly.

"Kirk's getting to sound just like you," she said, "always talking about religion."

Kirk was not only testifying at home, but he was talking to some of his pals in the sixth grade at Jefferson School about the Lord Jesus.

"How come you don't get mad anymore?" Guy Allen asked him as they left the football field at the close of recess. "When Freddie Bauer tackled you so hard a couple of minutes ago that you lost the football, you just grinned at him."

"I'm a Christian now," Kirk said. "I'm trying to live the way that Jesus would have me live."

"Huh?" Guy asked.

"You come to Sunday school with me next Sunday," Kirk went on. "And you'll find out all about it."

"Sunday school?" Guy echoed. "Not me. The guys in our neighborhood play football every Sunday morning. I can't miss that."

He told some of the rest of the guys about Kirk at noon, and they started to call him "the little missionary."

"It's tough, Danny," Kirk said that night as the two of them sat together in Danny's room. "Those guys get something like that going and they never know when to quit."

"You can take it, can't you?"

Kirk nodded grimly.

Danny knew what it was like to have to take it too. The football team lost another close game because of poor quarterbacking, and everyone blamed it on him.

"If Orlis wasn't such a religious fanatic," one of the guys said, loud enough for him to hear, "we'd be headed for the state championship."

"That's right," someone else added angrily.

Danny brushed on past them, his face flushed and his ears burning.

One thing that Kirk had trouble with was arithmetic. He had just squeaked by the year before, but up to now he had been failing this term.

"That's not a very good testimony to get grades like that," Danny said to him. "Why don't you bring that book home and do some studying on it?"

"We've got a whopping big test coming up," Kirk said. "The teacher told us that it is going to count an awful lot on our grades. Would you help me?"

"You bet I will."

Kirk had never studied very hard. But now he brought home his arithmetic book, and he and Danny spent an hour or two pouring over it every evening.

"We don't want to forget to pray about it either," Danny said the day before the test. "That'll help just as much as studying."

"I have been praying about it," Kirk said seriously.

The test went easily for him, and he wasn't at all surprised when he got his paper back in a few days and saw that he got an A+.

"Boy, that's a gyp if I ever saw one!" Guy Allen said to him. "Imagine you getting A+ in arithmetic."

"Surprised, aren't you?" Kirk laughed.

Miss Jones, the sixth-grade teacher came up behind him just then. "Kirk," she said coldly, "I'd like to speak with you a minute."

He went back to her desk with her.

"You know that you got a surprising grade in arithmetic," she said.

"I studied like everything."

"I hope that's true." She paused a moment. "A copy of the arithmetic questions for this test was missing two days ago. This looks very suspicious, Kirk."

"But I didn't steal those questions, Miss Jones," he protested. "Honest I didn't." He stopped as he saw the look on her face. She didn't believe him!

ELEVEN
Framed!

"But, Miss Jones," Kirk Barber protested, "I didn't cheat on my arithmetic test. Honest I didn't. But I did study awfully hard, and Danny Orlis helped me."

"You can scarcely expect me to believe that, Kirk," she said stiffly. "You've been doing failing work since school started. Now you suddenly get a perfect grade on your test."

Kirk started to tell her about taking the Lord Jesus as his Savior and wanting his testimony to be good in school and all of that, but he stopped short.

She gathered up her books.

"I want you to know this, Kirk. We're going to get to the bottom of this."

"I'm telling you the truth."

"Then you have nothing to fear," she retorted.

He walked out of the schoolroom, white faced and shaken. Guy Allen was standing on the steps.

"What's the trouble, Kirk?" he asked, grinning.

He started to speak, then stopped, and hurried quickly down the steps.

"That does sound bad, Kirk," Danny said when he told him what had happened.

"She said that she was going to get to the bottom of it," the young Christian said. "I don't know what she'd have to find to make her think that I was cheating."

"That isn't important right now," Danny told him. "The main thing is whether you did or not."

The following morning Kirk got up early and did his work around the house so that he could get away by ten o'clock to play football. Jefferson School was playing Walt Hill, and he was a starting end.

"I'm sorry, Kirk," Mr. Humphries, the janitor at Jefferson, who always refereed their games said to him, "but Miss Jones sent word that you aren't to play today."

Kirk's face turned crimson, and he hurried away before any of the guys could ask questions. He bit his lower lip savagely.

Back at the Barber home Danny helped Mrs. Barber clean out the basement and carry out the ashes. "I don't know how we ever got along around here without you, Danny."

He emptied the waste basket from under the sink and burned the papers, then went upstairs and changed into his "cords" and sweater.

"I think I'll go over and see Rick Haines."

On the way over to Rick's he met Kay going to the grocery store.

"I just talked with Marilyn," she said, "and she told me that she and Rick have a date tonight. They're going to a movie, but if you can get him to come to our party, she said she would come."

Danny grinned crookedly.

Rick was in the back yard tinkering with a small hand tractor when Danny stopped to talk with him.

Rick didn't even look up.

"Would you like some help?"

"You can if you want." His voice was cold and distant, but he let Danny help him attach the snowplow to the front of the tractor.

"I earn my spending money with this thing."

"Sounds like a great idea."

They sat there for a few minutes, talking about different things, until finally Danny said, "Say, Rick, how about coming to our Young People's party tonight?"

"Can't do it. I've got a date."

"Bring her along."

"I don't think she'd like it," Rick said disinterestedly. "Besides, there's another couple going with us."

"How about coming to our regular meeting, then?"

Rick got to his feet and started to push the tractor away. "I'll tell you, Danny," he said, "I'll start to come when you start playing football."

They had a fair turnout for the party, but only one of the people they had been praying for showed up. Kay was discouraged.

"I was hoping the party would really bring the kids in," she said.

"Remember what you told me?" Danny laughed. "You've got to keep on trusting."

"I guess we'll just have to keep praying that much harder," she replied.

"I agree with you completely, Kay," he said, "but I'm beginning to get some ideas of my own about this Young People's Society." He paused a moment. "We're building our group solidly, and that's the most important thing. But I believe we ought to do a little more for them when they get to the meetings."

"What do you mean?" she asked.

"Oh, I don't mean a big, fancy program, but if we could have a good, lively Bible study led by someone who really knows his Bible, it ought to help a great deal. Then I think we ought to have some games and a time when we really have some fun."

"It's something to pray about."

Friday night they lost another close game, and Danny met Mr. Cartwright on the street the following morning.

"Well," his former employer said angrily, "we lost again. I hope you're satisfied."

Kirk had been worried all weekend about going back to school Monday morning. But he had to go, and he had to face Miss Jones. There was no getting out of it.

Usually he and Karen walked together, but this time he toyed with his breakfast until she went on without him.

"You've got to hurry, Kirk," his mother scolded.

At school Guy Allen was waiting for him in the hall. "Boy, are you in for it!" he whispered. "Mr. Brown and Miss Jones have already been up and down the halls twice looking for you."

Kirk gulped.

In the principal's office Mr. Brown closed the door and had him sit down across from them.

"This is very serious, Kirk," he said. "I suppose you know that."

He nodded.

"Miss Jones tells me that you deny taking the list of questions from her desk, and cheating on the examination, Kirk."

"I didn't cheat," he said quickly.

The principal took off his glasses and slowly laid them on the desk. "Kirk," he said, "we'd be inclined to go easy on you if you were telling the truth. But we have evidence that you're not."

He took a crumpled sheet of paper from his pocket and handed it to Kirk.

"We found this in the bottom of your desk." The boy's face blanched white when he saw it. It was a copy of the arithmetic test in Miss Jones' handwriting!

TWELVE
A tough spot

"What do you have to say for yourself, Kirk?" Mr. Brown asked.

The young Christian stared at the crumpled paper.

"Do you think you're ready to tell us about it now?" the principal persisted. "How did you come to take the questions?"

"I didn't take them, Mr. Brown," he replied firmly. "I never saw that paper until right now."

He moistened his lips with the tip of his tongue. Danny would probably call upon God to help, if he were in his place. Kirk tried to pray, but he just couldn't. He felt so bad that somehow he couldn't find the words to pray.

"Well, Kirk," Mr. Brown continued, "we're waiting."

"I don't know how those questions got in my desk," he answered, "but I didn't put them there."

Mr. Brown took off his glasses again and wiped them thoughtfully.

"Well, Miss Jones," he said, "if Kirk isn't going to cooperate with us, we have no choice in this matter."

Miss Jones dabbed at her eyes with the corner of her handkerchief. She was crying.

"Kirk," the principal said, "until such time as you are ready to come to us and tell us how you got the test paper and when, you will be required to stay out of school."

Kirk got to his feet and stumbled blindly out of the office.

"What did they do to you?" Guy Allen asked. He had been waiting at the end of the corridor.

Kirk tried to speak, but he could not. He pushed past his friend and almost ran out of the school building.

Danny would be in school now and probably in class, but Kirk had to see him. He was almost home, but he turned and hurried toward the high school.

"I don't know," the girl at the desk said doubtfully. "We don't usually call anyone out of class during regular school hours."

"But I've got to see him."

"Well," she said reluctantly, "if it's an emergency."

"Say, now," Danny said sympathetically when Kirk told him what had happened, "that's tough. Have you got any idea of what you're going to do about it?"

The younger boy shook his head.

Danny pulled at his ear thoughtfully.

"I thought maybe if you went back to school with me, Danny," Kirk suggested, "and told them how I studied the week before that test, maybe it would help."

Danny got a pass for the morning and joined Kirk on the front steps.

"I'll send for Miss Jones," Mr. Brown said when they entered his office.

Kirk squirmed nervously and Danny, looking into the stern face of the grade-school principal, prayed silently for guidance and strength.

"I presume that you came here to tell us about the stolen test questions, Kirk," Mr. Brown began when the sixth-grade teacher had entered the office.

Kirk gulped hard and shook his head. "I–I brought Danny here to talk to you," he managed.

"I hardly know what to say," Danny began. "Kirk told me what happened and—"

The principal was drumming impatiently on his desk with a pencil. "Yes?" he asked as Danny paused.

"I room at Kirk's house."

"I know you," the principal broke in. "You're the fellow from Colorado who could be winning us some football games if you hadn't gone religious all of a sudden."

The color drained from Danny's face.

"I—I—" he began.

"Come on," the principal said impatiently, "let's hear what you have to say."

"I happen to know that Kirk did study awfully hard for that test. He brought his book home, and I helped him with his arithmetic for four or five nights in a row."

"The question is," Mr. Brown retorted, "did he take a copy of the test questions from Miss Jones' drawer?"

"I didn't," Kirk protested.

"I think you boys are wasting our time. You had just as well go back to your class, Miss Jones."

"I'm sorry, Kirk," the teacher said, her voice choking. "I'm terribly sorry."

She had started out the door when Danny stopped

her. "Just a minute," he said, "I just thought of something."

"We're very busy, young man," Mr. Brown told him.

"Kirk didn't have very good grades in arithmetic, did he?" Danny asked.

"He was failing."

"If he stole those questions, he would just have worked on the problems in the test, wouldn't he?" he went on.

"I suppose so."

"There wouldn't be any point in a guy studying all of his arithmetic if he knew the questions that were going to be asked, would there?" Danny continued.

"I don't see what that has to do with this matter," Mr. Brown put in.

"Would it be possible to give him another test?" Danny asked. "If he failed it, you would know that he had stolen the questions. If he passed with a real good grade, you would know that he had earned it."

"I don't know," the principal said hesitantly.

"He was doing failing work," Miss Jones agreed. "When I saw how good he had done, I suspected him of having taken the test paper."

"Well, I'm turning the matter over to you, Miss Jones," he said slowly. "You know about Kirk's work, and whether or not he would be able to pass another test. If you want to give him a test, it's up to you."

"You come in after school tonight, Kirk," she said.

When Danny and Kirk were finally outside, Kirk turned to Danny. "Boy, thanks!" he said fervently.

For a long while after Danny got back to school, he sat in the library, staring at the ceiling. The Thanksgiving game was coming up and already the kids were beginning to post "Beat Danville" banners in the halls, and soap slogans on the windows uptown.

"We'll skin Danville without Danny Orlis," one pep club member wrote on the jewelry store window. They had wiped it off in an hour, but not before Danny and half the kids at school had seen it.

He still squirmed when he thought of it. How could he make any friends at school when the kids felt the way they did? How could he win any of them when they looked at him as a fanatic and a poor sport?

Kirk went home and tried to study, but he couldn't get his mind on his arithmetic. His reputation, his Christian testimony, and his grade in arithmetic depended upon that test. If he failed it, or just squeaked by, he'd never be able to convince anybody that he hadn't stolen those questions. He went up to his room and knelt to pray.

At three o'clock he went back out to the school and waited until classes were dismissed.

"I've got the questions ready for you, Kirk," Miss Jones said as he entered the room. "You just sit down. I'll be back in a moment. I want to check them with Mr. Brown."

Kirk sat down weakly and waited.

Guy Allen and a couple of other guys were standing out in the hall, looking in at him and whispering. He knew what they were talking about. He just had to get a good grade on that test!

Miss Jones came back presently. "Here are the questions," she said. "You may take as much time as you wish."

Kirk took the test and looked at it. They were the toughest questions he had ever seen!

THIRTEEN
Just in time

Kirk Barber stared desperately at the test questions that lay before him. Sweat moistened his forehead and the palms of his hands.

He had never seen arithmetic so tough. Miss Jones was looking at him, eyeing him carefully as she pretended to be correcting papers. He knew what everybody would think when they learned that he had flunked this test.

"Lord Jesus," he prayed silently, bowing his head, "I can't work these problems. Please be with me and help me. I—"

As he prayed, the door behind him opened hesitantly.

"M–Miss Jones," a voice stammered. Kirk turned to see Guy Allen standing there, his cheeks ashen white and his lips trembling. "Yes," she said, getting to her feet the way she did when she was annoyed at being interrupted.

"I'd like to talk to you a minute," he went on.

"You may see me in the morning," she told him.

"But it'll only take a minute," he persisted.

"I don't have the time to talk with you this afternoon, Guy," she went on. "I'm giving Kirk this test, and I'll be busy until after five."

"Kirk shouldn't be taking that test," Guy blurted.

"What do you mean?"

Guy had advanced toward the front of the room until he was standing before the teacher's desk.

"I—I—" he began. "I took that examination paper."

"What?"

"I took the paper," Guy repeated. "Kirk didn't."

The words seemed to come out in a torrent as he told how he had found the paper on her desk that evening after school, and had taken it without realizing how wrong it was.

"I just wanted to get a good grade," he managed. "After I finished with it, I stuffed it in Kirk's desk. He didn't even know it was there."

Miss Jones came back to Kirk's desk.

"I–I'm awfully sorry," she said softly. "We should have known that you were telling the truth."

"That's all right," he said. He looked up at Guy gratefully. God had answered his prayer, all right, but how sorry he was for his friend.

"Both you boys may go now," Miss Jones said at last. "We will want to talk with you in the morning, Guy, but you needn't stay any longer tonight."

Kirk got awkwardly to his feet and walked out of the room and down the steps. People would know now that he hadn't stolen the questions, but what about Guy? His heart ached for him. Impulsively he stopped on the sidewalk and waited.

"Thanks," Kirk said, when Guy came out.

"I didn't plan on doing it," he said reluctantly.

Kirk looked at him as they walked together to the bicycle rack. If only he could find the words to convince Guy that he needed Jesus as his Savior!

"You talked to me about sin and giving my heart to Jesus until I couldn't sleep anymore after I'd done it," Guy said. "I never did feel so wicked about anything I'd done!"

"Jesus has the answer, Guy," Kirk said. "He's the One who can save from sin."

Guy got his bike out of the rack and stood for a long while holding it. "I know," he said finally, "but there are some things that I don't understand."

"I don't know if I can answer them or not," Kirk replied quickly. "But I know a friend who can."

"I don't want to talk to anyone," Guy protested, throwing one leg over his bike.

"But Danny's a great fellow," Kirk said. "He can answer the questions you have, and show you how to get right with God—how to take Jesus as your Savior."

The two boys talked for a moment or two, then got on their bikes and rode off up the street to find Danny.

Later that evening Danny told Kay what had happened as they sat in a booth at the ice cream shop sipping malts. "And so here came Kirk," he said, "with this other little fellow to be led to the Lord."

"It's wonderful," Kay smiled.

"He meant business too," Danny went on. "He said that he was going right home and tell his folks and his brother."

"What do you think they'll do with him at school?"

"Kirk wants me to go with him to talk to the principal in the morning," Danny answered. "I'm sure they'll be easy with Guy."

There was a long silence. Danny finished his malt and stared out into space for a moment or two.

"What are you thinking, Danny?" Kay asked softly.

"I was thinking about Kirk and Guy," he said. "You know, I tried to alibi for myself, and make up reasons which would show that I was right in wanting to work on Sunday and all that. And it's certainly been hard not to, especially with people feeling the way they do about me in town. But Kirk found the Lord, and now Guy, because I finally decided to place God's will first in my life."

She nodded, smiling. "That's the way it always is," she said, "when we decide to live completely for him."

THE DANNY ORLIS ADVENTURE SERIES

Tyndale House Publishers, Inc.
Wheaton, Illinois